"I've only dug out half this hole,
but broken my new spade!"

WITHDRAWN FROM STOCK

WITHDRAWN FROM STOCK

KU-590-351

It's tired Bull the dozer:
    he can't move the pile of rubble!

Bull stops and sighs. "It's just no
good. I *cannot* shift this earth."

"I've revved and revved
and pushed and
strained for all
that I am worth."

"I see the problem!" Fixer says.
"Your power's running low.
I'll swap your battery out for mine.
There! Have another go."

"I feel like **new**!" says Bull.
"I could lift ten thousand tons!"

"Glad to help,"
Fixer says,
and, tired,
he rolls on.

Here's Gertie grabber gazing
at an unmoved pile of rocks.
"I cannot grab a single one.
I've broken my gearbox!"

Have mine," says Fixer, reaching in
and handing her his own.
"First gear is enough for me and
it's time to head back home."

His spare-parts box is empty now,
his battery almost flat.

There's nothing more
to do, he thinks.
Oh well, I'd best head back.

But high above,
a single rock slides
from the mountaintop ...
And starts a landslide down the slope
that simply can't be stopped.
"What's that? A storm?"
says Fixer, as he
hears a thunderous

CRASH!

He wakes to find
    he's buried deep.

His metal treads
    are broken.

His grabber's badly
    twisted and his little
        engine smoking.

He hopes someone will find him,
    but slowly fills with doubt.
His battery fails . . .

        and one . . . by one . . .

                his little lights . . .

                        . . . go out.

But luckily for Fixer all his friends are rolling home,
When they find their path is blocked
by several hundred tons of stone.

One of Fixer's broken treads
is pinned beneath the rubble.

"Oh no!" cries Dug.

"Quick, help!" says Gertie.
"Fixer is in trouble!"

"Don't panic, everybody.
I can shift these rocks," says Bull.
"I'm big and strong and, luckily,
my battery's nearly full."

HEAVE.

Bull heaves the rocks aside
but finds only soil and sand.
"C'mon, Dug!" he cries. "Get over
here and lend a hand."

So Dug the digger's spade bites down
and soil flies through the air.
The hole grows quickly big enough –
they see poor Fixer there.

"He's down too deep," says Dug. "I can't reach him with my spade."

"Then step aside," says Gertie. "This is just why I was made!"

Her telescopic grab extends right down into the pit.

She s t r e t c h e s, says, "I'm . . . nearly . . . there . . . "
Then suddenly, **"THAT'S IT!"**

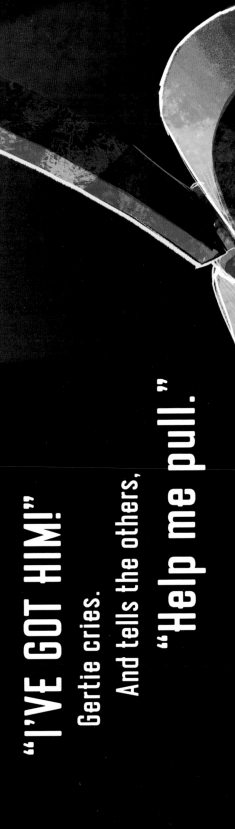

"I'VE GOT HIM!"
Gertie cries.
And tells the others,
"Help me pull."

So Fixer's dragged
out from the hole
by **Gertie, Dug**
and Bull.

Fixer wakes up back at base
surrounded by his friends.
They smile and say, "We're glad
to see you're finally
on the mend.

"Robots came from miles around when
they heard that it was you.
They said, 'Here, take this part! It is
the *least* that we can do!'"

Fixer grins. "My battery's full.
These treads are good as new!

...But I can't lounge
in bed all day.
There's work for
me to do!"

So every morning, Fixer robot
trundles up the hill,
To help the other robots as they
dig and push and drill.